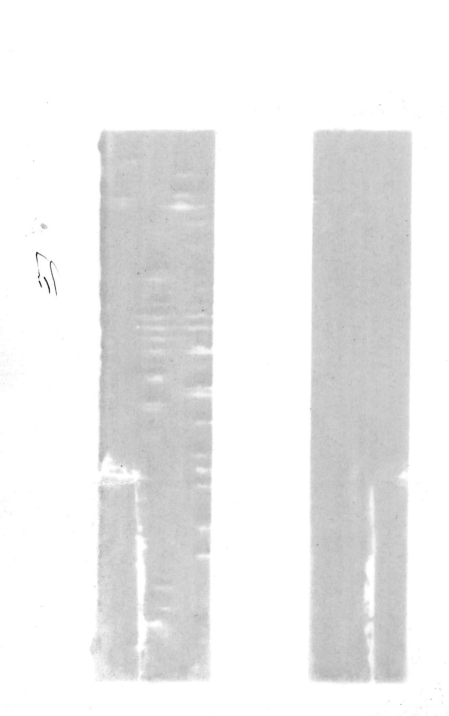

THE PICNIC

Ruth Brown

THE PICNIC

DUTTON CHILDREN'S BOOKS

New York

Rabbit sat bolt upright in the field, his ears quivering.
He sensed danger.

Humans! Rabbit and his friends raced for cover.

Underground, the animals gathered close together
as the footsteps echoed louder and louder above them.

Suddenly everything went black.

Mole, who was used to finding her way in the dark,
burrowed up through the earth and clay to investigate.

Something was blocking the rabbit hole. Mole pushed it aside.
Blinded by the sudden light, she blinked and sniffed.

Mouse, climbing up beside Mole, looked out…

and saw that danger was very near!

Mouse shot back down the hole, pulling Mole along
in a mad escape.

Behind them, the daylight shining through the hole suddenly disappeared. Instead there was a nose and a pink tongue...

and some sharp teeth and a pair of scrabbling claws that sent dirt and mud flying everywhere. Then, between the dog's paws, water gushed into the hole.

It was rain! Big drops drummed the earth, driving away
the dog and his people.

When the sun came out again, the animals went back
into the field and had a picnic of their very own.

For Glenn

Copyright © 1992 by Ruth Brown

All rights reserved.

CIP Data is available.

First published in the United States 1993 by
Dutton Children's Books,
a division of Penguin Books USA Inc.
375 Hudson Street, New York, New York 10014

Originally published in Great Britain 1992 by Andersen Press Ltd.

Printed in Italy   First American Edition
1   3   5   7   9   10   8   6   4   2
ISBN 0-525-45012-2